Captain Abdul's

PIRATE
SCHOOL

Books by the same author

Captain Abdul's Little Treasure

Jolly Roger

Making Friends with Frankenstein

*There's an Awful Lot of Weirdos
in Our Neighbourhood*

Who's Been Sleeping in My Porridge?

Wish You Were Here (And I Wasn't)

Captain Abdul's

PIRATE
SCHOOL

For Rocky Lawson,
the first pirate I ever met

First published 1994 by Walker Books Ltd
87 Vauxhall Walk, London SE11 5HJ

Sprinters edition published in hardback by Heinemann Library,
a division of Reed Educational and Professional Publishing Limited,
by arrangement with Walker Books Ltd

This edition published 2017

2 4 6 8 10 9 7 5 3 1

© 1994, 2001 Colin McNaughton

The right of Colin McNaughton to be identified as author
and illustrator of this work has been asserted by him in accordance
with the Copyright, Designs and Patents Act 1988

This book has been typeset in Garamond

Printed in Great Britain by Clays Ltd, St Ives plc

British Library Cataloguing in Publication Data:
a catalogue record for this book is available from the British Library

ISBN 978-1-4063-7874-0

www.walker.co.uk

Captain Abdul's
PIRATE
SCHOOL

Colin McNaughton

WALKER
BOOKS

Dear Diary,

Well, here I stinking am! My first stinking day at Captain Abdul's Pirate School. My stinking dad has sent me here because he says I'm a big softie! (Just because I like writing poems and painting pictures!) He says it will toughen me up. He says a kid my age should jump at the chance of becoming a pirate. He says that when he was a kid he wanted to be a pirate and so should I.

He says I should be grateful.

Well, I say, "Nuts!" and I say, "Steaming cowdung!" and I say, "I hope he swallows his pipe!"

P.S. I have a secret.

I have smuggled my little dog Spud in my trunk. He's the only friend I've got in the whole stinking world!

We were met at the door by
Captain Abdul himself: hairy,
scary and with more bits missing
than a second-hand jigsaw.

"Follow me upstairs, me little buccaneers," said Captain Abdul, "an' we'll get yer kit stowed away, ooh-arrgh, that we will. Ha-har, ooh-arrgh!"

Hammocks ~ ooh~arrgh!

Next we were given our school
uniforms and told to introduce
ourselves.

Jim
Silver

Françoise
du Plonk

Ching
Yih

Ali
Khoja

Unfortunately, Spud thought this included him! Luckily the captain likes dogs and said he could stay (for a small fee).

I was a bit nervous about meeting the other kids but they don't seem too bad – they look just as miserable as me.

Tom Tew

Anne Bonney

Frankie Drake

Samuel P. Chop

We then had supper and went to
bed, where I wrote this and cried
a bit for my mum.

Jack Rackam

Simon Smee

Ben Gunn

Mary Read

Beryl Flynn

Bartholomew
Sharp

Dear Diary,

Woke up this morning and stood up in bed. Forgot I was in a hammock – bit of a headache. I was brushing my teeth when Bully-boy McCoy came in.

"What yer doin' that for?" he asked.

Who ever heard of a pirate with nice teeth!

"If I don't, sir, my teeth will go black and fall out," I replied.

"What's wrong with that?" he said. "Who ever heard of a pirate with nice teeth!" And he confiscated my toothbrush!

Today we studied history.
Portobello Billy told us an exciting
story about Calico Jack the pirate,
set in his favourite place –
the West Indies.

Dear Diary,

We were queueing for breakfast this morning when Walker the Plank came over and asked Rosemary Lavender if she was pushing in.

"Yes, sir," admitted Rosemary.

"Well done!" said Walker the Plank and walked away.

Today's lessons were maths and geography. In maths we learned about angles. (You use them when aiming cannon.) In geography we learned where the West Indies are and how to read treasure maps.

Dear Diary,

The beastly Captain Abdul has scolded me for being too neat and tidy. He suspects me of brushing my hair –

"Combs an' hairbrushes, the possession of, is a floggin' offence, ooh-arrgh!" he told me.

Today we had arts and crafts. We learned how to make cannon balls, swords, fake money and how to put model ships into rum bottles. (Spanish Omar Lette very kindly emptied the bottles for us.)

Dear Diary,

Last night we were doing our homework when Riff-raff Rafferty came in and caught little Simon Smee copying from another boy.

"Was you cheatin', boy?" howled Riff-raff.

"Yes, sir," said Simon Smee in a small voice.

"Good boy!" yelled the teacher. "Go to the top of the class!"

Today we learned how to speak pirate. Can't wait till next week's lesson. It's pirate swearwords!
Ooh-arrgh!

Dear Diary,

The teachers had a party last night! They kept coming up and saying it was much too early to be in bed and why weren't we having a midnight feast or rampaging round the town looking for trouble!

"Why, when I was your age," said the captain, "I already had a wooden leg! Ooh-arrgh!"

When he finally woke up today he bellowed, "Fresh air is what we need, ooh-arrgh! We're goin' to sea!" For the rest of the day we sailed around the harbour in the *Golden Behind*, learning pirate stuff.

Dear Diary,

Tricked! Betrayed! Duped! Fiddled! Fooled and double-crossed! Last night, after I'd taken Spud for a walk, he ran into the staffroom and I followed him in.

From the shadow of the captain's hammock, hidden by clouds of tobacco smoke, I heard terrible things…

"KIDNAP!" I yelled, when I got back to our quarters. "Captain Abdul and his dirty double-crossing teachers are going to kidnap us tonight and when our mums and dads arrive tomorrow for parents' day, all they will find will be a ransom note! We must do something!"

45

"But what?" asked the kids.

"MUTINY!" said I. "We get them before they get us!"

"YES!" everyone shouted.

"Shush!" I hissed. "Get your swords and follow me. Tom, you bring the ropes."

"Aye-aye, Captain!" said Tom. "I mean, yes, Pickles."

Armed to the teeth with swords
and ropes, our fearless band of pirate
pupils crept down to the staffroom.

I gave the order and we attacked!

The battle was over in minutes. We swarmed all over the pirate teachers and tied them up with so much rope they looked like cocoons!

We rolled the teachers out onto the quayside.

One of the kids shouted, "What now?"

"We sail for the West Indies!" I cried. "Who's with me? Who really wants to be a pirate?"

"ME! ME! ME!" they all shouted.

"Good!" said I. "Raid the kitchen,
fill the water barrels and get the
ship ready. We sail in ten minutes!"

I wrote a note to our parents
telling them what had happened,
pinned it to Captain Abdul and
we set sail.

Dear Diary, (six months later)
This is the life! We now call
ourselves "Pirate pirates" because
we only steal from other pirates.
On our last raid we found out that
pirates from all around the world
had heard about our mutiny.

Thinking how well taught we must have been, they have sent their kids to Captain Abdul's school! Abdul claims the mutiny was all his idea – part of his teaching plan. The scoundrel!

And so everybody is happy: Captain Abdul because his school is a roaring success and our parents because we send lots of treasure home.

The kids are happy because they get to sail and swim and fight and fire cannon and rob bullies and stay up all night!

And me? Well,
I paint my pictures
and write my poems
and I'm captain of
my own pirate ship!
Who could ask for
anything more…

I'm Captain
Maisy Pickles –
the happiest girl
in the whole, wide,
wonderful world!